NANNY SEX COLLECTION

EXPLICIT DIRTY EROTICA SHORT STORIES

ERIC RESHER

plicit Press

CHAPTER 1

COMBUSTION

CAYCE WRIGHT HAD a thing for his eighteen-year-old babysitter and his wife Joanne knew it.

Ashlee Carver was every man's masturbatory fantasy: long white-blonde hair, cloud gray eyes, and killer curves. More than once, Cayce had found himself aching and hard after watching Ashlee blending over to care for baby Patrick. It didn't matter if it was her firm round ass in tight shorts or the view of her full breasts down the front of her shirt. Either way, Cayce constantly had to excuse himself to the bathroom where he'd jack off, all the while picturing covering her cherubic face with his cum.

It had been during one of these moments that Joanne Wright had entered their bathroom with her usual swagger and made a proposal he couldn't refuse.

Mr. Wright was totally a DILF, in Ashlee's humble opinion. Late twenties, dark brown hair, and topaz eyes. True, he was a bit on the short side, but Ashlee had seen him in just a pair of shorts, and, damn, he had a better body than most of the guys in Ashlee's class at the tiny Florida high school where she was a senior. Six-pack and smooth skin. A bulge that Ashlee bet would turn into at least an eight or nine-inch cock.

So, when Mr. Wright called her into the backyard to tell her that Patrick had gone with his grandparents and invited her to take a dip in the pool, how could she say no? Especially considering how yummy he looked in his black swim trunks with water cascading down his sun-kissed skin.

Ashlee felt a shiver go through her at the sight of those topaz eyes darkening as she pulled her t-shirt over her head. She knew her 42DDs looked good in her black lace bra and made a point of shimmying from side to side, as she slipped off her shorts to reveal her matching thong. With a giggle, she dove over Mr. Wright's head, entering the water with hardly a splash. When her head broke the surface a minute later, he was right behind her.

"Oh, Mr. Wright," Ashlee laughed. "You startled me." She put her hands on his shoulders, grinning when he sucked in a breath. "Seems like you want to do more than startle me." "Is that an offer?" Mr. Wright's hands slid around her waist.

"Fuck, yes," Ashlee brushed her lips over his, taking the opportunity to press her breasts against his chest, her nipples hard bullet points straining against the wet fabric. She ground her hips against him, eliciting a groan. "How do you want me, Mr. Wright?"

"All fours," he didn't hesitate.

Ashlee's grin widened. "Why, Mr. Wright, you've thought this through."

· · ·

He slid one hand down her back to knead her ass. "I want those pretty tits to swing while I fuck

you."

Ashlee writhed against his body, feeling his hard length press against her stomach. She was wet and it had nothing to do with the pool. She let him walk them back to the side of the pool and lift her up onto the edge. She took a moment to appreciate his strength before moving over to the towel that'd been laid out by the pool.

She got down on her hands and knees, and tossed a glance over her shoulder, watching Mr.

Wright climbs out of the pool. He caught her eye and hooked his thumb in his waistband. He winked at her as he yanked his shorts down. His cock sprang up, hitting his flat abs. It was as thick and long as she'd thought, and her pussy throbbed in anticipation.

He knelt behind her, running his hand over the smooth skin of her ass. The tip of his cock brushed against her as he leaned over her back, reaching for the clasp of her bra. Ashlee heard him groan as her full breasts were freed, the straps sliding down her arms. He cupped the flesh and she moaned, the heat from his palms spreading through her body. She wiggled her ass in a blatant invitation.

"What're you waiting for, Mr. Wright?" She kept her voice breathless, knowing full well the effect it would have.

He released one breast, rolling the pale rose nipple with his other set of fingers.

· · ·

"Put it in me, Mr. Wright," Ashlee was going to explode if he didn't fuck her. She whimpered as she felt him pull aside the nearly non-existent crotch of her thong. "Yes," she hissed as the tip circled her entrance.

"When he shoved himself home, she keened, fingers digging into the towel under her hands. He was so much wider than her two previous lovers, reaching places she hadn't known could be reached.

With one last tweak of her nipple, Mr. Wright's hands moved to her hips and began to pound into her at a bruising pace. She yelped with each thrust and wondered for a moment at the picture they painted.

Joanne Wright slid her hand beneath the waistband of her pants, unable to take her eyes off her husband and the babysitter. Ashlee was wailing, face contorted in ecstasy as Cayce's dick drove into her, his hips swiveling on every other stroke. Joanne knew exactly what the girl was feeling, the way Cayce's girth would stretch her so wide it felt like her pussy would split in two. The blonde's breasts swung free, jiggling each time Cayce moved and Joanne had the sudden urge to suck on them, to take all of one wide nipple into her mouth.

"Fuck," Joanne swore as her fingers worked her to climax.

A few feet away, Cayce pulled out of Ashlee and stroked his cock, his cum spurting out over her back. When he crouched lower and buried his face between the girl's cheeks to make her climax, Joanne came again, remembering the feel of her husband's tongue in her pussy, around her asshole.

Ashlee apparently found Cayce's oral ministrations to her liking as well. Her body slumped to the ground, limbs shaking.

Cayce sat back on his heels, face glistening in the late afternoon sun. He looked over at the pool house, his eyes locking with hers. Joanne could almost feel the heat from his gaze. Oh, yeah, they were so doing this again. And, this time, Joanne fully intended to get her own piece of that young, firm ass.

CHAPTER 2

BABYSITTER SLUTS THE GOING RATE...

WITH FOUR INTERVIEWS lined up for this afternoon, Tim isn't too happy that his wife, Michelle, is still stuck at the office. He gets through the first two very slowly, hoping that she will arrive. But at the end of the third interview, she sends him a message to say that she won't be home until later and that he should just get through all the interviews and they would discuss them later.

This pisses him off a little more than it should. But he's also had a long day.

He pours himself a drink while waiting for the last girl, a young college student called Ruby. Her picture on her application is simple; no makeup, and hair in a neat bun, thin-framed spectacles on her face. This is exactly what she looks like when she rings the bell and Tim lets her in. Ruby is dressed in a comfortable dusty pink cotton summer dress.

When she sits down Tim goes to the questions on their list immediately, making notes. His eyes have noticed that the dress has gone a little too far up the pale girl's thighs, revealing intricate freckles all the way up her legs. She crosses her legs and Tim can see that she definitely works out.

Ruby uncrosses her legs when she notices Tim's eyes on her legs. Then she crosses them again, drawing his eyes again and again. When his eyes have settled, and he is starting to stutter through his questions, Ruby parts her legs ever so slightly and casually lets her dress move a little further up her thigh. Tim is, after all, a very attractive forty.

He doesn't need to question what is going on. Ruby is clearly opening up a gap that will speed up the interview and ensure that the job is hers. Tim is tired. So the idea of ending this interview quickly and decisively is appealing. His cock agrees with him completely.

Tim checks his watch as he moves toward Ruby. He runs a finger along the side of her face and then gestures for her to follow him. They go to his study, which will be the last place his kids would come looking for him, knowing that it is off-limits to them. Ruby's clit starts its rhythmic pulses as she watches Tim's ass as he moves. He, too, obviously works out.

He pushes her against the door and locks it. Her hands work on his buckle and his pants drop to his ankles as he lifts her dress. He pulls her panties down just a little bit and then whips his dick out of his trunks. The elastic settles almost too tightly under his balls.

Tim runs a finger along Ruby's full lips, wishing they were somewhere else so that there was enough time for him to put her mouth on his cock. Fuck, it's a beautiful little mouth. But he needs to make this quick. He knows already that he is going to hire her and so there will be other opportunities to move his cock between her lips. His model-like wife would never expect him to be attracted to this plain Jane.

His cock isn't small. But Ruby's cunt is. He towers over her and so he takes her hands and puts them on his dick. He whispers for her to put it in herself. She takes the massive dick gently and directs it between her legs. She gets onto her toes and then lets Tim move into her in an easy, carefully calculated stroke. She grabs his arms as her cunt starts to stretch in every direction.

Tim checks that she can take it. She begs him to go deeper. He knows that she is just being ambitious and so he continues to enter her tight little pussy slowly. Then he pulls out a little before going back in some more. Her cunt is tight and a little drier than it should be if he is going to get all the way up in there. There just isn't time for this easy-does-it approach.

He pulls his cock from inside and pulls her to his desk. He lifts her onto it and pulls her panties off completely. She is on her back and he goes down towards her pussy with his mouth. After giving the clean-shaven pussy a few licks, he drops a blob of spit directly onto her hole. Then he stretches her cunt briefly with two fingers. He gets more spit onto her cunt and then uses his fingers to spread this makeshift lube on the inside of her pussy.

As soon as his fingers slide all the way inside her there is no more time to waste. He pulls Ruby off the table so that she is standing again, her hands holding onto the side of the table. He positions his cock himself and moves it into her cunt. It's still tight, but one firm thrust gets more than half his dick inside the interviewee.

He moves in and out of her slowly at first, begging her to loosen up but hoping secretly that she wouldn't loosen up too much. Lucky for him, there is no way that Ruby could loosen her tight pussy even if she tried. Even as she starts to produce her own moisture, her cunt is a beautiful, hugging force that is the object of every cock's deepest fantasy.

Tim keeps going. Ruby whispers huskily for him to go even deeper. Her dress has fallen over where his dick is digging into her so he can't see how deep he has managed to go already. He hates that he is missing out on these visuals, but there's just no time now to make this into a movie.

He grabs Ruby under her ass and gets her back onto the table. He pulls her close and he manages a few more inches into her. She wraps her legs around him and pulls him even deeper. Tim groans a little louder than he would have liked. He looks at the many screens on his desk that allow him to monitor his house from his study. The children are still having their afternoon naps.

He goes harder. With her legs gripped around Tim's strong body, Ruby arches back; and after pulling her dress up, she holds the fabric gathered against her breasts so that she can move her hands across her nipples over and over again. Tim's gratitude results in an even harder dick and a series of deeper thrusts. Fuck there is nothing like young pussy.

His eyes are glued to where his thick, almost rosy meat is going for gold. He pushes the fleshy parts of Ruby's cunt deep into itself and then pulls them back out. Each thrust adds to the sweat beading on her forehead. Her hair too has started to stick to her face. They hadn't noticed that it has come undone.

Tim lifts her off the table and continues to fuck her as he makes for a wall. He pushes her hard against it and then thrusts even harder up and into her. As he does this, he pushes her down firmly on his cock. He lifts and lowers her over and over again until her cunt gushes a river onto his groin. She was just so fucking hot for him that she couldn't hold back. But now her cunt is wet and Tim won't cum quickly inside it even though it is still considerably tight.

He carries her back to the desk, lifting her off his dick and turning her over. He parts her ass and drops some spit where it's needed. He takes her hand and places it on his dick, willing her to put it in. She positions the dick where it needs to be and then moves back and forth until the head finally goes in. Then she lets go and holds on to the edges of the table within reach.

Tim bends lower and takes hold of her upper arms. Then he drops his cock into her ass and is challenged more than he expected by the tightness he finds there. But he goes for it, Ruby pressing her lips tightly together so that she doesn't make any more noise than she already is. Tim thrusts his way all up inside her butt and then gives but a moment's pause for her to breathe.

Then he takes himself home. He moves his long shlong all the way in and then out. All in and almost all out, he repeatedly sinks into Ruby. She braces herself against him but takes every inch that he drives into her. She starts to grind her butt in tiny circles to speed things up. She isn't naïve to the urgency of the situation. Soon enough they are working together perfectly and Tim knows deep inside himself that he is almost done. Again, he checks the surveillance screens.

He pulls Ruby away from the table just a little bit more. Then he reaches under her for her pussy. It is still dripping. He digs into it easily now with a few more fingers. Ruby appreciates it so much that she wraps her asshole even tighter around his dick, and makes her circles even bigger. All Tim can manage now is harder thrusting. But his fingers in her cunt make Ruby very accepting of Tim's pipe in her asshole.

Ruby has another orgasm and Tim starts to get anxious. He moves his fingers from her pussy and places them on her back. Because of the perfect humps, he manages to push her back and forth at will now on his dick. His thrusts are vicious now, his orgasm impending. He moves his hands onto her ass cheeks and spreads them so that he has a maximum view of his dick disappearing and reappearing in her tunnel.

Then he goes all the way in and grinds in wide circles of his own. Ruby takes an arm and puts it under her face so that she can sink her teeth into her own flesh. This is the only way that she can keep herself silent. Everything about this cock in her ass feels awesome. But she usually needs some time to warm up to dicks half this size. There won't be this luxury today.

Tim is really getting all the way inside her ass now as he gets closer to the end. His thrusts slow down slightly so that he can align his orgasm perfectly with the throbbing inside every muscle inside his dick. This is the only way that he will be able to control the noises that usually escape him when he fucks fast and with abandon.

Eventually, his balls contract as his cock starts to pump its load into the tiny freckled behind that he is piercing. He goes all the way in and makes a deposit. Then he pulls back just a little to reload his bazooka. Tim thrusts all the way back in and deposits some more of his heated load. He repeats this a few more times until he is satisfied that his cock is empty.

They make their way from his study and straight to the front door, Tim confirming that he will discuss the details of the interview with his wife and be in touch. Ruby knows that there will be a few details missing from this discussion.

Michelle is really late getting home. This is a good thing

because Tim doesn't need to explain to her why he is in the shower when she arrives… She joins him. And Tim can take his time working his dick inside every hole of this body that he is actually allowed to have. Ruby crosses his mind a few times, Michelle's cunt quite formidable in its own right.

Fortunately for Tim, it doesn't take too much convincing to get Michelle to agree to Ruby. Tim can now work out just how and when he is going to get those perfect lips sliding up and down his cock…

CHAPTER 3

BABYSITTER SLUT (YOU'RE NOT MY LITTLE SISTER!)

WHEN MR. and Mrs. Johnson finish getting ready for date night, they're already late for their reservation. Fortunately, Ivy, their reliable sitter is already engaged in a very elaborate tea party with their pride and joy, seven-year-old Emily. In the rush, they forget to tell Ivy an important bit of news. But it isn't long before the sexy, nineteen-year-old African American cheerleader finds out for herself.

Emily is warm, snug, and fast asleep dreaming of unicorns and mermaids less than an hour after her parents have left. Ivy relaxes into the plush sofa in the TV room, watching the first of the films she brought to keep herself occupied until 2AM, which is when she is expecting the Johnsons back. But there is a faint sound coming from the gate, the sound of it opening. There are only four homes in the plush complex, so one of the other families must be having a late night.

But then she hears a key in the door and she looks around to see what it is the Johnsons could have forgotten, probably a purse or a coat. But there's nothing. She stands up, wrapping the blanket around herself and walking towards the door, the key sounding a little stuck on the other side. She gets onto the balls of her feet just to take a precautionary peek through the peephole before unlocking the door. Just as she does, the door swings open, pushing her back into the entrance hall and down on her bum. The person who walks in is neither Mr. nor Mrs. Johnson...

"You're not my little sister...," says a surprised but almost stoned-looking Adonis. He looks like a bigger, handsomer, male version of the little girl asleep upstairs, but nothing like her parents.

"And you're not mine..." Ivy says, mocking him, relaxed by the fact that there is a family portrait in the entrance hall and the young man in front of her, no older than she is, looks like an older version of the youngster standing next to Mr. Johnson. This must be the infamous rebel, Tyler.

Tyler bends over and reaches for Ivy. She takes the hand offered. He lifts her off the floor with a force that sees the blanket fall from her shoulders and leaves her in her tight tank and track pants. Tyler pulls her closer to himself and smells her menacingly before introducing himself. She introduces herself, understanding from just this smell, and the odor of rum and cigarettes coming from him, that everything she's heard about why he is at a military school is absolutely true.

He drops his duffel and locks the door. They walk to the kitchen and Tyler piles leftovers onto a plate. For a second Ivy wants to offer to help but then decides that this boy is in his home. She excuses herself and escapes to the TV room again to finish her film. She isn't forgetful of her blanket in the foyer.

She's barely resettled and Tyler is in the TV room sitting closer to her than he should considering they've just met. He eats loudly and mocks the romantic comedy on screen. But when an unexpected sex scene lights up the screen Tyler is suddenly quiet. In the three minutes that the soft and mostly suggestive visuals on the large plasma screenplay out, Tyler finishes his food without realizing it, saying nothing throughout.

He pulls the half of the blanket closest to him off Ivy and covers himself as he puts the plate that was hiding his erection on the floor. His hands move to Ivy and he realizes that she is inaccessible, sitting on most of the blanket. She looks at him with both a question mark and an answer, checking her wristwatch to see if there will be time enough to make an intimate acquaintance with Tyler's dick.

"No strings buddy, just fun..." Ivy speaks to him with mock authority. "Just the way I like it...buddy..." He mocks her right back.

She gets up and then under the blanket with him. He moves his hand under her tank immediately, going all the way up to her breasts and rubbing them roughly. Ivy loves the intensity of his touch. He climbs on top of her, straddling her lap as she sinks deeper into the couch, still sitting. He tries to lift Ivy's top off and she stops him. She explains the impracticality of it. They lower the volume on the TV so that they can hear any movement in the house, remembering Emily.

After a quick shuffle, Ivy is on her back, lying down. Tyler is on top of her, kissing her hungrily, filling her mouth with the taste of gherkins and mayonnaise. She doesn't mind, her pussy wanting to be stuffed with the dick that is rubbing against it and part of her flat belly.

Ivy pulls her pants and panties down below her ass so that Tyler understands the urgency. He totally gets it, pulling his own pants almost to his knees. Then he pulls Ivy down a little further, to her taut calf muscles. Again, she

cove that is reeking of the sex they haven't even had yet. He lowers his waist so that his dick is touching her face. She tries to get it in her mouth with his help but eventually she has to bring her hands up to take hold of this long cock. Then she guides it between her lips, Tyler already back on her pussy with his own mouth.

He has to move his legs lower down so that they are separated by Ivy's shoulders because his dick is struggling to create the path to her throat that he yearns for. She lets his meat press hard against her tongue as she eases it into the back of her mouth. He lifts it out of her a little and then glides it back down, a little deeper. Then he lifts it out until just the head of his cock is wrapped between her lips. She licks the tip slowly and then wills him back down into the back of her throat.

Ivy creams again as Tyler's tongue works a little more rapidly on her clit and the inside of her pussy. She sucks hard on his cock as he brings her to orgasm after orgasm with just his mouth. He fucks her mouth as hard as she is sucking, building the steam inside his dick to take on this pussy, and hopefully her ass, that he is grooming for a hard pounding. As soon as his dick coats the back of Ivy's throat with its first load, he is ready to fuck the shit out of her. She is just as ready.

Tyler removes his dick very slowly and gives Ivy a moment to clear the dome and then the ridge where his foreskin once was of his excessive semen. Then he moves so that he is on top of her and their faces are touching. He can't resist kissing her as he positions his dick between her legs and searches for her snatch. It's fiery, as hot on the outside as Tyler knows it will be on the inside. She moans loudly as the length of Tyler's dick fills her cunt and makes its way all the way up inside her.

Now that he is in this hot heaven, he uses the muscles in his thighs and ass to move his cock around inside her. He isn't thrusting. It is almost as if he is using his dick to build an image of the inside of Ivy's pussy. He searches left, and then right, and then lower down, and then around and around. His dick goes everywhere, familiarizing itself with every part of this wicked vagina.

Tyler continues this searching, this dipping, and grinding until his cock is convinced that it isn't dreaming. Then he shuffles a little so that he has a clear path down into Ivy that crosses clear through her g-spot on every thrust. She can hardly breathe as Tyler starts to cut her spot in a million pieces with his dick. He hits it on every thrust, going hard, going deep, and going at it over and over again as though he was trying to carve it into tiny slivers just for fun.

Ivy's hands are on his ass, pushing him even deeper into her pussy. She matches his lust thrust for thrust. Tyler doesn't even try to compete. He doesn't try to be the man, proving his ability to fuck. He just feeds her every inch of his long, thick dick, soaking up the sounds coming from her each time he slices through her g-spot.

He fucks her like this until the room goes black, the screen running faint white closing credits. This signals that they've eaten into their alone time considerably and that they need to finish. Tyler really starts to pound her now. He fucks her wildly on the expensive couch that doesn't make a sound. He watches her face, checking how close she is. When he sees that she has arrived, he drives his dick into all the parts of her pussy that need it so that her banks are burst and she has a raging orgasm, wetting her ass and much of the sofa. Thank god it's leather.

Then he turns her over and goes straight into her ass. She raises her bum so that he goes deep quickly. He grabs her from underneath and places his palms on her thighs. With his eyes closed now, he rides Ivy's tight asshole with all the power in him, his orgasm making a full and final occasion of the tiny ring, stretching it wide as gallons of hot, wet, cock-juice pump from Tyler's balls, through his shaft, and into Ivy's chocolate box.

By the time the Johnsons arrive home, Tyler and Ivy are all cleaned up, as is the sofa. Tyler is asleep in his bedroom, and Ivy is half asleep on the sofa, her third film almost done. They leave her to sleep and go upstairs to check on their children. Ivy is already dreaming of tomorrow night...

CHAPTER 4

BABYSITTER SLUTS
DINGALING DONG!

"I'LL TRADE you this pizza for your pussy..." Rico speaks English as though he were speaking Spanish. His accent is thick and his tone husky, making him as much of a treat for babysitter Trisha as the pizza he is carrying.

She isn't sure if he's joking, using crass humor to secure a tip. So for the sake of her pussy, which is flaming already between her legs just at the sight of the new guy, she pulls him into the apartment where she has already put the ten-year-old twins she is babysitting to bed. This pizza was to be her midnight snack, the twins were not allowed any junk food, and so she had to wait until they were in bed to order it. This is the only rule her bosses have.

Rico can't believe his luck. Usually, he has to try this line for at least three visits before the woman he wants to bone realizes that he is serious. But he can tell in Trisha's eyes that this girl isn't like other American women. In fact, he learns very quickly that she isn't even American. Fortunately for Rico, Trisha is an English exchange student who just happens to have 'get super fucked by a hot Latino' on her list of things to do in the States.

They tiptoed up the stairs and past the twins' bedroom. Trisha checks in just to be sure. The pair is fast asleep. She leads Rico up the stairs to the guest cloakroom just off the second-floor landing. It will be easiest to clean should there be an accident. Also, one seldom needs an excuse to be in a locked bathroom, should one of the girls wake up.

By the time they are safe inside Rico's dick feels like it is set to burst. He mumbles a few words and Trisha shuts him up with her palm over his mouth while she gets his pants undone. She frees his dick in the dark, the light making her feel exposed and paranoid that funny noises could result in juvenile eyes peeking through the keyhole. Then she is on her knees, kissing the thick, uncut cock all the way up and down the shaft. It's a fucking impressive piece of equipment.

She nibbles on the meaty foreskin, enjoying the fact that Rico tastes of sweat and cum. He has probably been cumming a little in his pants all night, dripping a little each time a sexy woman opened the door to him. This is the moment he had been hoping for all night. Trisha's tongue finds the underside of his foreskin and traces circles around the rim of his dick's perfectly shaped tip.

Then her mouth is on it. Rico can't see his dick disappear down her throat. But who the fuck cares about seeing what you can feel? And boy can he feel it. Trisha gets all the way down to the base of his Latino pipe and pulls on his pubic hairs with her teeth as she slides her mouth back up. She leaves the dick wet and cold for a second as she again enjoys the tastes that nestle just under his foreskin. Then her mouth warms Rico's cock beautifully as she slides back down and fills her mouth completely with cock.

She sucks on his dick while putting her fingers inside her own panties and warming her clit. She digs into her pussy as it wets itself, her mouth wetting Rico's dick as much as she can without soaking it. She wants him inside her fast so that there is enough time for his dick to run the ambit of her cunt before she kicks him out. Rico just closes his eyes and holds onto the sink, letting himself be used any way Trisha wants to.

When she is happy that her pussy is ready to take this thick rod in one move, she stands up and pulls Rico to the toilet. She closes the lid and gets on her knees. Rico pulls his pants all the way to his ankles so that he can kneel comfortably behind her. Trisha adjusts the mat on the floor so that their knees don't hate them when they're done.

She covers the toilet with a large hand towel, and then rests her head on the soft terry, trusting that Rico will know what to do now without being told. He does. Rico spits into his hand unnecessarily, probably the reflex of a man who knows that he has too much dick. He wets the tip of his cock and then spits into his hand again, rubbing this second blob onto Trisha's cunt as he forces her legs a little wider apart.

He runs the tip of his dick over her clit as he moves in closer behind her. Holding his cock, he draws slow circles over the surface of the flower before searching for the entrance to her pussy. He finds it with ease and then holds her back as he slides his cock into her throbbing vagina. She takes him all in one go.

Rico massages Trisha's ass as he begins to thrust slowly yet powerfully all the way into her English muffin. Trisha lets herself be moved back and forth, as her pussy is plunged over and over again. Thanks to the towel, she glides easily over the porcelain surface of the toilet lid.

.   .   .

She twerks her ass like she was born in Brooklyn and this drives the Latino crazy. He bites into his fist and she knows that she has impressed the delivery guy.

After about ten minutes of acquainting himself with Trisha's pussy, Rico can either bring it to a close or take her cunt on a trip along the scenic route. He is too nervous to ask in case she asks him to finish up. Trisha just keeps pulling his dick in tight circles with every muscle in her pussy, unaware of the questions he is asking himself. It takes Trisha a few more minutes to bring herself to a very controlled orgasm, thanks to the thickness of the cock inside her and Rico's not letting his indecisiveness affect the consistency of his strokes.

Trisha pushes back on him so that he knows she wants him to move back. He does, crawling backward as she pushes against him, keeping his dick inside her. When she is free of the toilet and on all fours, she gives him a few more twerks before abruptly ejecting his cock from her pussy. Rico panics. But then she lifts him to his feet and seats him on the towel covering the closed loo. He smiles in the dark, knowing exactly what is coming.

It's clear that the English Channel is not as cold as they said it was back in high school. Trisha's pussy is on fire as Rico holds his dick upright so that she can slide her cunt onto it while she straddles him on the toilet. She settles completely onto his lap, his dick completely inside her.

She reaches behind him with one hand, grabbing the window's security grill. Her other hand grabs the rail against the wall next to them. With this firm brace, she moves her cunt up most of his cock and then drops it down completely. Each time she settles on him completely Rico moans, not sure whether he is cumming or just in heaven.

It's a rare treat when a girl treats you to her pussy.

American chicks usually just let the guy do the work. This is something Rico will hold onto for a long time, this chick who took his dick on a trip to Britain minus the visa and cold weather. He's definitely not going to charge her for her pizza.

Trisha moves with some serious commitment up and down on Rico's dick as he rubs his face over her covered breasts. He manages to expose them and take them into his mouth as she works on his cock, needing no input, save for the maintenance of his erection, from him. She starts to move in circles once she has him all the way inside her again. He practically bites into her tits from excitement. Trisha loves the feeling of his teeth threatening to pierce her flesh.

Her circles become more and more intense. She is not moving up and down the taut shaft but moving around and around on it. Rico sinks even deeper between Trisha's firm breasts, parting them with his face. Then he fills his mouth with the perfect tits while Trisha's cunt pulls every inch of his dick so deep into itself that Rico feels like his cock is bigger than it is. And it's already fucking huge.

There is no way for Rico to involve himself now as his dick is being ridden by this ferocious filly. Trisha's feet are firmly on the floor so that she can brace herself against the dick that has completely stuffed her. She pulls on his dick in every direction using nothing but her pussy and the power she packs in her thighs. It's the first time that Rico has ever been able to completely lose himself while fucking. He imagines that this is the kind of experience that one has with an older woman. But Trisha is three years younger than he is. He doesn't know this though, this conversation is not one they've had. They've had no conversation at all really, their genitals doing all the talking required.

Then Trisha wraps her arms around Rico. She does the same with her legs. The circles become impossible so she grates her cunt back and forth, milking Rico's dick mostly from the base. It's more than enough for Rico. His cock is so amped now that his erection seems to reach out in every direction, completing Trisha's sense of fullness as she fucks Rico with incredible persistence.

He tries as hard as he can to thrust up into her, succeeding only marginally. But Trisha has such power in her little body that she takes him from level to level so that he feels that he is getting close to his own orgasm. He is practically intoxicated by this delicious pussy taking him to places he knows but in a way, he has never traveled before.

Rico can't take this pleasure anymore, his dick unable to handle this passenger seat suddenly. He throws his hands around Trisha, holds her to him, and then stands up. She is surprised by this move and squeezes her legs around him so that she doesn't fall. But he has her locked in place by his cock and his arms so that she isn't going anywhere.

He moves her onto the basin counter so that her ass is perched precariously on the edge. But still, she is wrapped tightly around his body so that there is no way that his cock will slip from where it is. Now Rico is the one thrusting, taking control of the final stretch so that he can lead his cock to climax at will. He needs this final sense of control. But he also wants to thank Trisha for her cunt by bringing her to another intense orgasm.

This is what he manages to do with but a few deep strokes. Trisha is surprised when tears roll down her face along with the wetness flowing from her pussy. Her cunt has taken more than it had been prepared for but Rico has made every single second magic, even in the moments when he did nothing. But now he needs to cum and so he shifts his focus to himself once he is sure that Trisha is completely satisfied.

He begs her for a few more minutes of her time, kissing her on her neck and lips as he thrusts repeatedly into her while holding her in place. Rico drives his cock into Trisha in a straight line now back and forth, all the way inside her as his cock starts to pulsate and reach its impending finale. He shoots into her cunt, flooding it with himself just before he meant to pull out. But it's too late, and he coats Trisha's cunt with spicy Latino jizz and touches his head to hers as he has a totally satisfying orgasm.

After she confirms for him that she is vigilant about contraception and such, they exchange numbers and make a tentative appointment for the next weekend.

CHAPTER 5

THE BABYSITTER MAKES THREE

MY WIFE and I desperately needed a night out on the town. We had a one-year-old and we hadn't done anything fun in almost a year besides going to a few movies. For a couple of nights, we ate out. We had planned a decent outing tonight. We were going to have dinner at our favorite steak house and then go see a live performance on stage. We were very excited about it. So I left early to go pick up the new babysitter, Chelsea. She was a 20-year-old college student that came highly recommended.

When I drove into Chelsea's driveway, I honked like she said on the phone. I was a bit taken aback when she walked out to the car. She was smoking fucking hot for one thing. She had long dark hair and a body I could spontaneously cum too if I thought about it hard enough. When Chelsea got into the car, I was even more attracted to her. She smelled great and I could see her pussy. She didn't have any panties on and she spread her legs on purpose so I could get a good look at her furry quim. Her pussy looked good enough to eat and fuck right here on the spot. She playfully placed her right hand under her skirt to let me hear the juicy noises coming from deep inside her hole.

I felt my dick growing in my pants and pressing up against the zipper. It ached to be fucked or sucked by this hot chick. I resisted even though I wanted her so fucking bad I almost groaned out loud. Then I started fantasizing about me, my wife, and Chelsea getting it on back at the house.

Suddenly Chelsea seemed like a more exciting adventure than going to a live production. She was a flirty little cunt too. She kept looking over at me and my cock. She even reached over one time and grabbed my package. I damn near squirted off.

We pulled into the driveway and as Chelsea kind of swung her legs around to get out of the car, I smelled her pussy very distinctly. It smelled perfectly ripe and raring to get fucked. I actually considered going to the john and rubbing one out after that. When we went inside my wife was looking pretty fucking hot too. She had big tits and Chelsea and I both could see her big bulging milk-filled tits pressing through her sheer mint-colored top. I know my wife and she looked like she had been masturbating. She had that horny glow on her face. And when I stepped in closer, I knew my assumptions were right. I could smell her delicious cunt as well.

I guess it was just sex in the air because we were all ripping our clothes off before we knew what was happening. Chelsea latched onto one of my wife's tits and started sucking her milk out. I had never seen another woman suck my wife's tits before and especially not seen them drink her creamy milk. It drove me to the point of a pre cum squirt from my bell pepper-shaped cock head. All women loved the feel of my bulbous head against their g spots when I banged them. They usually squirted every time my rim grazed them inside their cunts. I stroked longer and slower dying to pop inside of Chelsea and bang her to the wall. That is exactly what I did too. My wife kind of lifted her ass onto me and then I put her back to the wall and I fucked Chelsea's brains out. My wife humped her hot ass with her furry blonde snatch. I saw my wife's cream all over Chelsea's butt. Fuck that was enough to make me pop off one good time, but I knew I had more in me, and I still needed to eat two pussies at once.

After slowly pulling out of Chelsea's drenched cunt she went down on it real fast and drank her own pussy juice off of it. Then she let my wife eat her cunt off of me. They kissed me and smelled like pussy and that was just too fucking hot. They each lay side by side on the floor and I went to town eating snatch. I fucking adored bushy pussy and they both had a bush extraordinaire. My wife was blonde and wavy and Chelsea's was black and silky. It felt good tickling my nose as I buried my face in her.

Chelsea asked sweetly if she could eat wifey out. We both said a harmonious yes! As Chelsea buried her gorgeous face in my wife's bush, I made a chain and buried mine in hers. Chelsea squirted a wad of pussy gush in my mouth and I swallowed every honey-flavored drop. As she was about to bring wifey to orgasm, I stood up and let the wife suck my dick off. She was deep throating me from the effects of Chelsea's nimble tongue upon her clit and hood. It stood straight out like a hard mini-cock. My wife started squirming and jerking as if she was having a seizure. The pussy eating must have felt fucking hot as hell is all I could say.

I timed my big load release to my wife's orgasm perfectly and Chelsea was fingering herself off again ferociously. It wasn't long before the three of us were moaning and practically screaming in all-out ecstasy. We had triple orgasms of the most intense kind. My wife and I were able to make it to the late showing, and we both could smell sex all over us for the remainder of our date. I wonder if my wife was thinking what I was thinking. I know I was thinking let's do the babysitter again baby. She is too hot for her own good. We got to the door and opened it up and there was Chelsea toying herself off butt naked on the kitchen table. Needless to say, she, my wife, and I had another amazing threesome before I took her home and she sucked my cock off hard on the way.

ABOUT THE AUTHOR

Eric Resher

Eric Resher is an emerging erotica author of many erotica kinks and sub-genres. Be sure to check out other books and leave a review if this story got you hot!

Visit my blog at Eric Resher Blog

Join my newsletter for the exclusive Eric Resher Newsletter

Sign up for Free Stories from Xplicit Press Authors

Xplicit Press Author Updates

Like Xplicit Press on Facebook

Follow Xplicit Press on Twitter

Readers: I want to expand a few of the stories to see where the characters can be explored further. If there are any of the stories that you would like to read more about again, I'd love to hear from you!

Keep In Touch
Eric Resher
info@ericresher.com

9 7 9 8 8 8 7 0 0 2 0 7 1